# HE WHO BELIEVES IN ME SHALL NEVER DIE

## GRACE DOLA BALOGUN

Copyright ©2013 Grace Dola Balogun

Contact Author at:
www.Gracereligiousbookspublishers.com
1-646-559-2533

Grace Religious Books Publishing & Distributors books may be ordered through booksellers or by contacting the publisher:

Grace Religious Books Publishing & Distributors, Inc.
New York
213 Bennett Avenue
New York, NY 10040

The author of this book does not dispense medical advice or prescribe the use of any technique as for treatment for physical, emotional, or medical problems without the advice of a physician, either directly or indirectly. The intent of the author is only to offer information of a general nature to help you in your quest for emotional and spiritual well-being. In the event you use any of the information in this book for yourself, which is your constitutional right, the author and the publisher assume no responsibility for your actions.

Soft Cover: ISBN# 9781939415189
Hard Cover: ISBN# 9781939415271


Library of Congress Control Number: 2013932172
Editing and Interior Design by CBM Christian Book Marketing
www.christian-book-marketing.com
Cover Design by Lisa Hainline www.lisahainline.com


Printed in the United States of America
Grace Religious Books Publishing & Distributors, Inc. New York

# DEDICATION

I dedicate this book to God the Father Almighty who spoke Jesus Christ His begotten Son into being as God's Word and wisdom incarnate.  Christ as the attribute of God the Father, just as our words and thoughts come from us and cannot be separated from us, in the same way Jesus Christ cannot be separated from the Father.  Christ as the Word of God, the Speech of God, Christ is the living Word of God who lives forevermore.  Christ is the wisdom of God and the power of God.

I also dedicate this book to those who will read it.  May they acquire great wisdom and knowledge in believing that in Christ the righteousness of God is being revealed from faith to faith.  They will live by faith to the point that they will give their lives to the One and only, the Word of God and God.  May they know clearly that Jesus Christ is the life; believe in Him and you will live forever; you will not die.  His power of resurrection will resurrect your spirit soul and body. You will be blessed with the immortality that dwells in the light, that no darkness can comprehend.

6

I also dedicate this book to all the people on Earth that seek after their own righteousness and finally one day they will come to the knowledge and understanding of the righteousness of God in their lives.

# PREFACE

Through their fall, the human race became independent of God and began to distinguish for themselves between good and evil. In this Earth of imperfect and perverted human judgment people decide what is good and evil. This was never God's will, for He intended in His loving kindness desired us to know only good in dependence on Him and His Word.

In this world all who confess Christ as their Lord and Savior return to God's original purpose for humanity. Believers rely on God's Word to determine what is good. Adam's perfect relationship to God had been lost. He was driven out of the Garden, into a life of dependence on God in the midst of trials. In addition, Satan gained power over the world through the fall of Adam and Eve; in the New Testament he is called the prince of this world. "I will not speak with you much longer, for the prince of this world is coming. He has no hold on me" (John 14:30).

Another Scripture says, "The god of this age has blinded the minds of unbelievers, so that they cannot see the light of the gospel of God" (2nd Corinthians 4:4). Here the Scriptures refer to Satan as the God of this age who holds power over much of the activity of this present age. His rules, however, are temporary and conditional. He continues only in God's permissive will until the end of history. Those he has blinded and who have not submitted themselves to Jesus Christ will remain under Satan's dominion. Christ is the glory of the Gospel to save the people of this world.

The solution to Satan's activities is through prayer and intercession, and through the preaching of the Gospel in the power of the Holy Spirit. In order that people in the world may hear, understand and choose to turn to Christ and be saved. "You will receive power when the Holy Spirit comes on you, and you will be my witnesses in Jerusalem and in all Judea and Samaria and to the ends of the earth" (Act 1:8). The primary purpose of the baptism in the Spirit is the receiving of power to witness for Christ so that the lost will be won over to Him, in that they will be taught to obey all that Jesus Christ commanded.

The goal is that Jesus Christ may be known, loved, praised as the Lord and Savior of all of God's chosen people. The power of the Holy Spirit means that the believer will obtain strength or ability and designated power, especially in operation of the things of the Lord, as well as in action of witnessing the Gospel and in actions to emphasize the Holy Spirit's power, which included the authority to drive out evil spirits and anointing to heal the sick as the two essential signs that accompany the proclamation of God's Kingdom.

The release of power of the Holy Spirit in the Book of Acts through the believers help them to witness with great boldness, and great power to testify with many signs and wonders and miracles, with proclamation concerning the believer's testimony of Christ's saving work of redemption and resurrection.

The baptism in the Holy Spirit not only imparted power to preach Jesus Christ as Lord and Savior, but also increases the effectiveness of that witness because of a strengthening and deepening relationship with the Father, Son and Holy Spirit that operate from being filled with the power of the Spirit. With the power of the Holy Spirit, we can live forever with the Lord from this Earth to Heaven. The Spirit of life will shed the love of Christ in our hearts and make us alive in Him.

Believers must totally surrender to Christ, which will result in living in union with Him forever. The gift of everlasting life belongs to all the believers of Jesus Christ. The believer will never die in spirit. Everlasting life is the believers' inheritance.

# TABLE OF CONTENTS

# CHAPTER ONE

## THE POWER OF GOD IN THE OLD TESTAMENT

From the Old Testament to the New Testament God demonstrated and exercised His power. He let us know that he created us to live forever with Him. Before the fall of Adam and Eve the Scripture says, "Then the man and his wife heard the sound of the Lord God as he was walking in the garden in the cool of the day, and they hid from the Lord God among the trees of the garden. But the Lord called to the man, 'Where are you?' " (Genesis 3:8-9). We can see clearly here that before the fall of Adam and Eve that they have a good relationship with the Lord God. The Lord God gave them everlasting life, to live eternally with God on this Earth.

One of the basic sins of humanity is the sin of unbelief in the Word of God. People of this Earth did not take God seriously, or they think that God can easily change in mind concerning sin. People always believe that God loves them, because God's love for them they feel that they can do whatever they want to do and still have God. They feel that God does not really mean what He says about salvation, righteousness, sin, judgment and eternal death.

"The Lord God made garments of skin for Adam and his wife and clothed them. And the Lord God said, the man has now become like one of us. Knowing good and evil he must be allowed to reach not his hand and take also from the tree of life and eat, and live forever" (Genesis 3:21-22). Satan's most persistent and continuous lie is that unrepentant spirit, and he will make them to continue in deliberate sin, and knowingly engage in what they know that which is not approved of God. Deliberate sin and rebellious character is against God. Human beings always seek to be independent from God by gaining moral knowledge and understanding with the power to determine what is good and what is evil in this world.

Adam and Eve committed the sin of disobedience and they were spiritually dead, immediately separated from God, while physical death flows. Spiritual and moral death happens up until today when people sin. Moral death consisted of the following: God's life in the sinner and thus nature becoming sinful. Spiritual death means that their former relationship with God was destroyed, resulting in a condition of guilt and condemnation instead.

Since the sin of Adam and Eve every person born comes into the world with a sinful nature. This corruption of human nature involves the desire to go on his or her own selfish ambition without concern for God, or others, and it was passed to all human races. Thanks be to God who sent His only begotten Son that whoever believes in Him will not perish, but have everlasting life. Lord God imputed the sin of Adam and Eve on Jesus Christ. Jesus Christ took on all our sins, and freed humanity. Those who believe in Him are free from the sinful nature and made them alive in Him. The Scripture said the last Adam, God, always cares for His people. For instance, concerning Adam and Eve, even though they sinned, therefore disobeying God's commandment, He corrected their disobedience, yet He does not disinherit them, but like a Father, He provides for their food and put coats of skins to cover their body. With this in mind, we have to acknowledge God's love with praises and thankfulness, not only for His provision of food and clothing, God made the coats of skins, very large and comfortable, strong and durable that fit them perfectly. It is the same with us today; God made the righteousness of

Christ to cover our past, present and future sins. Believe in Him you and you will not perish, you will have everlasting life in Him. The Scripture says, "Put on the Lord Jesus Christ so that you will not fulfill the lust of the sinful nature or flesh. "So it is written; the first Adam became a living being, the last Adam, a life giving spirit. The Spiritual did not come first, but the natural, and after that spiritual" (1$^{st}$ Corinthians 15:45-46). The faithful who are still alive at Christ's return for His followers will experience the same bodily transformation as those who died in Christ prior to the day of resurrection.

The Scripture tells us that Adam were created in the image and likeness of God from the dust of the ground, while Christ is the image of the invisible God. Jesus Christ was one through whom God created all things. "He is the image of the invisible God, the first born over all creations" For by him all things were created: Things in heaven and on earth, visible and invisible, whether thrones or powers or rulers or authorities; all things were created by him and for him" (Colossians 1:15-16). Christ Jesus is the heir of the ruler of all creation as the eternal Son. Apostle Paul affirms that creative activity of Jesus Christ.

All things both material and spiritual, owe their existence to Christ's work as the active against in creation.

In Christ all things are held together and are sustained in Him.

17

18

# CHAPTER TWO

## ENOCH WAS TRANSLATED TO EVERLASTING LIFE AND HE NEVER DIED

"Enoch walked with God, and then he was no more, because God took him away" (Genesis 5:24-25). There is no doubt Enoch excelled in godliness according to the Scripture. Enoch walked with God means he followed the commandment of Lord God. He loved the Lord God by obeying God's orders; moreover, Enoch lived by faith in God. He trusted in His Word and in His promises by making every effort to live a holy life that pleased the Lord God. He also embraced God's ways, while at the same time, he stood firm against his generation's ungodliness.

Enoch was a preacher of righteousness during his days on Earth. He denounced sin and any form of unrighteous life style of his generation. In the book of Jude, it was mentioned that Enoch prophesied and cried out against ungodliness and immorality, warning the people of his days of God's coming judgment to punish men and women for their ungodly deeds. Enoch was the seventh from Adam. He prophesied about these men, and said to them see the Lord is coming with thousand s upon thousands of His holy ones to judge everyone on earth, and to convict all the ungodly activities they have done in ungodly ways, and of all the harsh words ungodly sinners have spoken against Him.

We read in the Scripture that Enoch pleased God. His life, message and godliness was so pleasing to God that God honored him by taking him away from the Earth to be in His presence forever without experiencing death. Because Christ was still in Heaven, no one went to the third heaven until Christ ascended to heaven. Therefore, Enoch was taken to where he was able to get close to the Lord God at the second heaven, because God did not want him to see death.

Today everyone that belongs to Christ can never die because Christ has bought all those who believe in Him eternal life; they will never die. Believers today should ponder and copy Enoch's life as an example for we too live in an evil and ungodly generation. Believers today should walk with God to live in truth and holiness; believers should denounce sin and warn people to flee the coming wrath. As we want for Christ Jesus' return, when He will take us away from this earth where we will live with Him forever.

Enoch entered into second heaven without experiencing death implies that righteous men and women before Abraham's time possessed a hope for future life with God. The nature of Enoch's religion is that He walked with God. True religion and godliness, but walking with God, the ungodly and profane are without God in the world, they walk contrary, to Him, but the godly walk with God.

To walk with God is to set God always before us, and to act as those that are always under the eye of God. The best life is to live a life of communion with God both in ordinances and providences. Believers must try their best to make God's Word number one in their lives; the Word of God to must rule in our life with His glory reaching to our character and daily actions. Enoch was entirely dead to this world, and did not only walk after God, as all good men do, but what makes him unique unlike any others, is that he complied with God's will. He agreed and concurred with God's designs and pondered together with the Lord God. Enoch was on Earth, but was living as if he was in Heaven. He witnessed to people around him about the righteousness of God. Enoch walked with God with the power of the Holy Spirit for it is the life of a good man to walk with God. Believers should construct their lives to do what is pleasing in the Lord's sight in order to live with Him forever in Heaven.

Enoch was translated, which means transfer, transport, exchange, or change sides, or carried over. One of these happened to Enoch because he lived a clean and holy life that pleased God. Believers should copy the life of Enoch.

Enoch was delighted to listen to God. He communicated with God may be by dreams or through dreams, or by visions. Perhaps, Enoch even communicated to God through audible revelation. Enoch liked what God liked and hated what God hated. Enoch was one with God as Christ was one with God and as Christ was one with the Father. While other people denied the presence of God in their lives, Enoch walked with God. He always delighted in pleasing the Lord. With this in mind, nothing can be more comprehensive, or more and fully expressive than Enoch and God. Enoch set a right pattern for all the believers of Jesus Christ. Enoch humbly served the Lord God and he was transported to the second heaven awaiting

Christ's work of redemption to arrive.  Believers must do all they can in obedience to walk faithfully with God.

The word walk implies a steady progressive relationship, not just casual friend.  To maintain a good relationship with the Lord is a lifetime that believers need to develop and grow in.  This walk should become part of believer's daily life activities; it can never be on and off, today or the next day.  Enoch was transferred to the second heaven before the flood.  In the same way all believers will be raptured to Heaven before The Great Tribulation.

24

HE WHO BELIEVES IN ME SHALL NEVER DIE

# CHAPTER THREE

## ELIJAH WAS TAKEN TO HEAVEN IN A WHIRLWIND

"When the Lord was about to take Elijah up to heaven in a whirlwind, Elijah and Elisha were on their way from Gilgal. Elijah said to Elisha stay here, the Lord has sent me to Bethel" (2nd Kings 2:1-2). We see here that Elijah was taken to Heaven, as Enoch was taken to Heaven without seeing or experiencing death. It shows believers that whoever faithfully sincerely gives their life to God, God is always with them, with His power and mercy and loving kindness.

At the close of Elijah's ministry, he crossed back to Jordan to be taken up into Heaven. Elisha asked for twice the spiritual power of Elijah. Elisha was asking his spiritual father to give him an abundant measure of his prophetic spirit in order that he might be able to carry on the work of Elijah. God granted Elijah's request, knowing that the young prophet was willing to remain faithful to him and to God with all that was going on around the world at that time.

Elijah was taken to Heaven, the same as Enoch, without experiencing death. The miraculous transportation of Elijah to Heaven was God's emphatic seal of approval on Elijah's spiritual ministry. Elijah had been totally united to the Word of God throughout his ministry, faithfully serving the Lord God through His Word.

Elijah lived to the very end for the glory of God and honor; he stood against the sin of people and idolatry. Elijah encouraged the faithful who remained in Israel during his days. God greatly acknowledged Elijah's work; he was given a dramatic escort to Heaven in triumph. The transportation of Elijah encourages believers or prepared believers for the future rapture, catching up in the air God's faithful people when Christ returns.

God had determined to take Elijah up into Heaven by a whirlwind because God looked back upon Elijah's work and services, which he had done which were extraordinary. God decided to recompense Elijah, as well as to make it an encouragement to the young prophets after him so that they could follow in his footsteps of faithfulness.

God looked down upon this present dark world and the degenerate state of church, and gave believers a sensible proof that there is another life better than this present world. His plan and purpose is to draw the hearts of all the faithful believers towards Himself was revealed. He looked forward to the church's different denominations, evangelical dispensation, and in the transportation of Elijah, gave a type and figure of the ascension of Jesus Christ and the opening of the Kingdom of Heaven to all believers.

Elijah by faith was close to God by prayer communication with the heavenly Father and God wants him to live in Heaven with Him. Elijah lived his life to God while still here on Earth. Elijah determined to make God his all in all. Believers must follow Elijah's footsteps while they were here on Earth, for we know that we shall soon be with the Lord. The souls of all his people shall be happy there in Heaven forever.

The miracle of dividing the river Jordan was to prepare Elijah's transportation to the heavenly Canaan, as it had been the entrance of Israel into the earthly Canaan. God will take up His faithful people to Heaven; death is the

Jordan which, immediately before their transportation, they that must pass through, and they find a way through it, a safe comfortable way; by the death of Jesus Christ which divided those waters that the ransomed of the Lord may pass over.

The chariot and horses appeared like fire, not for burning, but brightness, not to consume him, but to render his ascension conspicuous and illustrious in the eye of those that stood and afar off so view it. Elijah had burned with the holy zeal of God and honor, and now with a blessing of heavenly fire, he was refined and transported. The chariot parted from the disciple on the day of ascension.

Elijah had once, in passion of fearing that he might die, hid in a cave during his service to the Lord; yet God was so gracious to him as to honor him with this privilege, that he should never see death the same as Enoch. God showed how men should have left or departed the world if they had not sinned, which is not by death, but by a translation. God gave a glimpse of life and immortality, which was brought to light by the Gospel through Jesus Christ, and through the opening of the Kingdom of Heaven to all the believers, as then which was offered to Elijah and Enoch.

This analogy could also be compared and made clear as a figure of Christ's ascension from the Earth to Heaven.  Christ Jesus was raised from the dead, afterwards for forty days, he was here on Earth with us before He was taken up to Heaven in the presence of His disciples and all His followers.  Christ ascended to Heaven and He will soon return to judge the people of this universe.

30

HE WHO BELIEVES IN ME SHALL NEVER DIE

# CHAPTER FOUR

## MOUNT OF TRANSFIGURATION SHOWS MOSES IN EVERLASTING LIFE

"But even the archangel – Michael, when he was disputing with the devil about the body of Moses, did not dare to bring a slanderous accusation against him, but said, The Lord rebuke you! (Jude 9). If the archangel Michael refused to slander Satan, but relied on God to rebuke him how much should we as human beings and believers of Jesus Christ refrain from presumption in attacking spiritual powers and authorities. Believers must at all times defend and propagate the faith and resist false teaching in four ways.

Believers must build themselves up in their most holy faith. The holy faith is the New Testament revelation handed down by Jesus Christ and the Apostles. It requires study of the Word of God, determining to know the truth and the teachings of the Scriptures as believers of Jesus Christ. Believers must learn how to pray in the spirit. By praying in the spirit, believers must pray by the enabling power of the Holy Spirit, looking to the spirit to inspire guide, energize, sustain and help them to do battle in their praying.

Praying in the spirit includes both praying with one's mind and praying with one's spirit.  Believers must remain in the sphere of God's love for all the people on this Earth.  This involves faithful obedience to God and His Word.  Believers must wait for God's return and the eternal glory that will accompany Christ's return.  "And Moses the servant of the Lord died there in Moab, as the Lord had said.  He buried him in Moab, in the valley opposite Beth Peor, but to this day no one knows where his grave is.  Since then, no prophet has risen in Israel like Moses, whom the Lord knew face to face, who did all those miraculous signs and wonders as the Lord sent him to do in Egypt to Pharaoh and to all his officials and to his whole land.

"For no one has ever shown the mighty power or performed the awesome deeds but Moses did in the sight of all Israel" (Deuteronomy 34:5, 10-12).  Moses was not allowed to enter the promised land before his death, however, after many years later Moses did enter it when he appeared on the mount of transfiguration along with Elijah and spoke with Jesus.

The Scripture says, "Just then there appeared before them Moses and Elijah talking with Jesus. Peter said to Jesus, 'Lord, it is good for us to be here. If you wish, I will put up three shelters one for you, one for Moses and one for Elijah.' While he was still speaking, a bright cloud enveloped them, and a voice from the cloud said, this is my Son Whom I love; with him I am well pleased. Listen to him" (Matthew 17:3-5). There was no prophet like Moses. Moses' great distinctions were his intimate fellowship with God and his understanding of God's nature and person. A believer's desire should be to know the Lord God and experience His close relationship; this should be our greatest privilege and our right as the children of God.

No believer of Christ, who possesses an inner life of devotion and an outer life of godliness, will be denied God's presence and grace. Believers will never be denied the fellowship of God the Father, God the Son, and God the Holy Spirit. This is the believer's greatest promise from Jesus Christ and greatest reward from the Lord God Almighty. Moses brought the Israelites to the borders of Canaan and then died; this signifies that the Law made nothing perfect.

The Law brings men and women to the wilderness of conviction, but not into the Canaan of rest that is full of wine, rubies and gold, and settles peace. It was reserved for Joshua and our Lord Jesus Christ to do that for us whom the Law could not do, because it was weak through the flesh. Through Jesus Christ, we enter into rest, in that we receive the spiritual rest of conscience and the eternal rest in Heaven. Moses' intimacy with God was incomparable; God knew Moses face to face, and Moses, as well, knew God. His interest and power in the kingdom of nature, the miracles of judgment he performed in Egypt before Pharaoh, and the miracles of mercy did in the wilderness before the children of Israel, demonstrated that he was a particular favorite of Heaven, and had an extra ordinary commission to act as he did on Earth.

Never was there any man whom the people of Israel had more reason to love or whom the enemies of the people of Israel had more reason to hate or fear. Moses was greater than any other prophet in the Old Testament. Even though there are men of great interest in Heaven and men of great interest on Earth, yet they were none of them to be comparable with this great man; none of them can be compared or either were so evident that executed a commission from Heaven as Moses.

God gave Moses the Law that molded and formed the Jewish Church by the other prophets by sending, or on a particular reproofs, gave directions and predictions. The last prophets concluded by changing the people of Israel to remember the Law of Moses. Scripture says, "He will stand and shepherd his flock in the strength of the Lord, in the majesty of the name of the Lord his God. And they will live securely, for then his greatness will reach to the ends of the earth. And he will be their peace" (Micah 5:4). Jesus Christ himself, during his earthly ministry, often mentioned the writings of Moses. Moses was a faithful servant of the Lord, but Jesus Christ is our Savior that ascended to Heaven and is sitting at the right hand of God.

# CHAPTER FIVE

## JESUS RAISED THE WIDOW'S SON TO EVERLASTING LIFE

"Soon afterward, Jesus went to a town called Nain, and his disciples and a large crowd went along with him. As he approached the town gate, a dead person was being carried out the only Son of his mother, and she was a widow. And a large crowd from the town was with her. When the Lord saw her, his heart went out to her and he said, "Don't Cry," then he went up and touched the coffin, and those carrying it stood still. He said, Young man, "I say to you, get up." The dead man sat up and began to talk, and Jesus gave him back to his mother" (Luke 7:11-15). Jesus Christ is the giver of life; he is the source of life. Christ has compassion for this widow. He showed His believers that God has a special love and care for all the people in the world, including widows and the fatherless, as well as for people who are alone or living a lonely life in the world.

Scripture teaches believers that God is a Father to the fatherless and a defender of widows. "A Father of the fatherless, a defender of widows, is God in his holy dwelling" (Psalm 68:5). Here the fatherhood of God for all the believers is emphasized in both the Old Testament and in the New Testament. God delights in protecting the weak, disadvantaged, the wronged and the lonely among His people. If anyone feels alone in this world, believers should pray for them and ask God to put them under his special care and protection day and night by means of God's provision for His people. God provides for the fatherless and the widow. Jesus saw that if the son died, the mother was a widow, there will be no one to care for the widow. He decided to raise the son of the widow back to life so that he can continue to take care of his mother until the mother is old and until she died.

God blesses those who help the lonely people; He honors them. Widows are recipients of God's tender love and compassion. Jesus Christ raised to life a widow's son at Nain. This miracle was wrought the following day after Jesus had cured the centurion's servant. It was done at a gate of a small town called Nain, which is not too far from the city of Capernaum.  Jesus Christ's miracles were always done in front of the crowd.  This particular miracle was performed and witnessed by two different crowds that me t by the gate of the city.

There was a crowd of the disciples, as well as the crowd of the people who were attending the widow's son funeral of the young son.  The young man that was raised to life by our Lord Jesus Christ was young, but the Scripture did not reveal his actual age.  He was the only child and the only son of his mother who was a widow.  This means that the father of the young man had died and the young man was the only surviving member of the family that could take care of this widow or his mother.

The mother depends upon his son to take care of her in her old age, but the young man died.  This brought a deep sorrow on this woman.  Jesus' sympathy for this widow draws a large crowd at the burial of this young man.  Everybody was condoling and comforting her for her great loss.  Christ showed up at the right time and at the right place and having pity on the widow, He showed His power by raising the man to life.

Jesus Christ showed His tender loving care and great compassion towards the afflicted then and He still does up even to today.  Jesus Christ is the same yesterday, today, and forever. He never changed. He will never change. When the Lord saw the poor widow following her son to the grave, He was full of compassion on her. Christ reached out to help this widow when nobody asked Him. The case of the widow was piteous, and Christ looked upon the widow with pity, and said: to her, "Weep not." What a pleasing moment and glimpse this gives to us believers today of the compassion of the Lord Jesus and the multitude of His tender mercies which never cease.

Christ said, "Weep not," for your dead son, for he shall presently become a living son. This case was peculiar to the widow, yet there is another reason which was common to all the believers of Jesus Christ who sleep in the Lord; that they shall rise again and they shall rise in glory, and therefore, the Scripture said, "We must not sorrow as those that have no hope" (1$^{st}$ Thessalonica 4:13). All the believers of Jesus Christ must let their passion at such a time be checked and calmed by the consideration of Christ's compassion. Jesus Christ has the power over sin and death, He command death itself to leave the young man.

Jesus Christ reached out and touched the coffin, and stops the funeral not to precede, the funeral procession stands still. How many times are people very sick in the hospital, and when people pray our Lord always puts a stop to the death sentence of the person and releases them to continued living. Jesus Christ with power and authority with solemnity and gentleness said to the young man, "Young man get up." Jesus Christ's power went along with His Word in order to return, or put life back into the young man. Christ Jesus' dominion over death was evidenced by the immediate effect of His Word.

He that was dead "sat up," another evidence of the young man being made alive is that he started talking; he began to speak. Whenever Christ made us alive in Him, by giving us spiritual life, He opens our lips in prayer and in praises to His Holy Name. Christ our Lord and Savior handed the young man back to his mother so that he can resume his duty as a son. Christ made him a dutiful son again, as well as giving him the gift of everlasting life in and through Him.

# CHAPTER SIX

## JESUS CHRIST RAISED JAIRU'S DAUGHTER TO LIFE

"When they came to the home of the Synagogue ruler, Jesus saw a commotion, with people crying and wailing loudly, He went in and said to them, "why all this commotion and wailing? The child is not dead but asleep". But they laughed at him. After he the put them all out, he took the child's father and mother and the disciples who were with him, and went in where the child was. He took her by the hand and said to her, Talitha Koum! (Which means, little girl, I say to you, get up)" Immediately the girl stood up and walked around (she was twelve years old). At this they were completely astonished. He gave strict orders not to let anyone know about this, and told them to give her something to eat" (Mark 5:38-42).

The daughter of the Synagogue Ruler had died, Jesus response was to encourage the father's faith, in this event, even if it is a seemingly hopeless situation. Throughout the redemptive history, believers have placed their trust in God even when it seems as if all hope was lost. In a time like this God gave the necessary faith and delivered His people according to His Word, will and purposes. Believers should keep up a confidence in Jesus Christ, as well as dependence upon Him, and He will do what is the best. Believers must believe in the resurrection of Jesus Christ and then be not afraid. Jesus Christ went to the Synagogue's ruler's home with a selected company where the child was. Christ decided that no crowd should follow Him, but his three disciples, Peter, James and John.

Jesus Christ raised the child to life. There was extreme love by friends and neighbors in the community. Therefore, everybody was moved by her death and her death drew a big crowd that caused everyone to continue crying very loudly and screaming. This showed the evidence that the child was truly dead by the time Jesus Christ arrived in the home. When Christ told them that the child was not dead, but sleeping, their laughing and scorning of Christ serves as the proof of Christ's miracle when the child was raised.

Jesus Christ put out those unworthy, and who were so ignorant in the things of God to witness the miracle, because they did not understand Him when He told them that the child was asleep. The child's parents were present to witness the miracle of God, which was designed for their comfort.

Jesus Christ raised the child to life by a word of power, and said –arise from the dead meaning, "I command that the girl should arise. The dead have no power to arise, but where the power of God goes along with the word of God makes it the effective authority of the Word. Jesus Christ works while He commands and works by the command, and therefore, Jesus may command what He pleases, even in commanding the dead to arise.

This is the Gospel of God that Christ came to the world to do the Gospel call to those that are by sinful nature dead in their trespasses and sins, and can no more rise from death by their own power, just as the Jairu's daughter was unable to rise from the dead until the power of life in Jesus Christ raised him up. The child as soon as the life returned to her, arose and walked.

Spiritual life will appear by our communion with Christ, walking with Christ and putting all our hope and trust in Him. In His Holy name we will be strengthened and follow Him.  All the people that have known us before when they see the life of Christ shining on us, they will give glory to the One and only the source of life.  Those who heard about believers of Jesus Christ how they are living in newness of life in Christ will pick up the Bible and be converted.  They will give their life to the Lord of life, who alone has immortality in the light.  They will joyfully and faithfully praise the giver of life, Jesus Christ.

Believe in Him and you will never die.  Jesus Christ said to the parents not to proclaim or mention what happened and how their child was raised to life because it was not the appointed time.  Jesus Christ did not have any interest in the popular acclamation of the people.  His mission was to concentrate and press on to the Cross.  Jesus Christ, our Lord and Savior, took care of the girl, but it appeared that the girl was raised not only to life, but to a good state of good health, that she had an appetite to eat her food.

This clearly shows that where Christ Jesus had given spiritual life, He will also provide food for the support and nourishment of it to eternal life, for He will never forsake, or be wanting in the work of His own hands. Christ will first keep safe those who come to Him by faith.

# CHAPTER SEVEN

## JESUS CHRIST RAISED LAZARUS TO LIFE

"Now a man named Lazarus was sick. He was from Bethany, the village of Mary and her sister Martha. This Mary, whose brother Lazarus now lay sick, was the same one who poured perfume on the Lord and wiped his feet with her hair. So the sisters sent word to Jesus Lord, the one you love is sick, when Jesus heard this, Jesus said, 'This sickness will not end in death. No. It is for God's glory so that God's Son may be glorified through it.' Then he said to his disciples, 'Let us go back to Judea. Our friend Lazarus has fallen asleep, but I am going there to wake him up. Your brother will rise again." Martha answered, 'I know He will rise again in the resurrection at the last day.' Jesus said to her, 'I am the resurrection and the life. He who believes in me will live, even though he dies, and whoever lives and believes in me will never die. Do you believe this? Take away the stone.' When he had said this Jesus called in a loud voice, 'Lazarus, come out' " (John 11:1-43).

When we suffer or are sick, it does not mean that Jesus does not love us. Jesus cares for all those who believe in Him and trust Him, as well as those who have strong faith in Him. Jesus loved Mary and Martha, and Lazarus their brother, the Lord Jesus had a strong friendship, affection and devotion to them. But still they experienced sorrow, sickness and death. It is the same with all believers today. We love the Lord and we have strong faith in him, but still we go through death in the family, rejection, persecution, afflictions and various sicknesses.

These troubles still and will continue to happen to God's faithful people and chosen ones of God. Many churches will have people like Mary persevering in a loving devotion to the Lord, Martha faithful in good deeds and Lazarus who was suffering and dying. Families like Mary will cry out to the Lord. Jesus Christ said that His delay is not for lack of love, mercy or compassion, but it is for the glory of God and His Kingdom and for the ultimate eternal good of the sufferers.

Our confidence must not rest or depend on what God is presently doing, but on who Jesus is in our life.

When Jesus Christ delays that means He is going to give the believer a great thing, something higher that what the believer has asked for, and also, He delays in order to strengthen our faith in Him, or to exercise His great power in the believers' lives.   A strong faith that had the dimensions, of depth and breath, sometimes Jesus' actions might appear to indicate that he was unconcerned by the believers' suffering.   However, according to the Book of John, John repeatedly emphasizes that Jesus loved the family Mary and Martha and all the believers that might be going through long suffering in that He also shared in their sorrow.   Jesus Christ's timing and divine purpose was different than the believers.   God's timing and His will, in the middle of our trials, may benefit us, and perplex us as well.

God answers us according to His great wisdom, perspectives and love.   For the person who believes in Jesus' physical death is not a tragic end, it is an entrance to abundant eternal life and relationship with God.  Jesus said, "Who believes in me will live forever," which refers to the resurrection of the body.  Jesus said, "Whoever believes in Me will never die," depicts the resurrection of believers, that they will never cease to exist.   They will have new bodies, which is immortal and incorruptible ones that cannot die or deteriorate, perfectly designed by God for the greater life to come and hereafter.

The sweeter mercies are those which are occasioned by trouble, let this reconcile believers to the darkest dispensations of God's providence, they are all for the glory of God, and, if God be glorified, we must be satisfied. The Son of God might be glorified thereby, as it gave Him occasion to work that glorious miracle, the raising of him from the dead.

Let this be a comfort to those whom Christ loves under all their grievances that the design of them all is that the Son of God may be glorified. Therefore, Christ delayed coming to them, that Lazarus might be dead and buried before he arrived. This will give Jesus the opportunity to give Lazarus a new life instead of repairing the body of sickness. God hath gracious intentions even in seen delays; even though Christ did not make haste to Lazarus, He has His divine plan and purpose that must be revealed through Lazarus. God always sets up His own plan for our lives, which is far more greater, and higher than we set for ourselves.

Jesus Christ will come to the aid of His people when the time to favor them according to His set time arrives. Jesus Christ called all believers his friends; He said to His disciples our friend Lazarus was dead. He then gives them the divine plan of the death of Lazarus; it is a divine plan that was set for the glory of God.

Those, whom Christ is pleased to call as His friends, are all His disciples as well. Death will not and cannot break the bond of friendship between Christ and a believer. Death cannot separate believer from the love of God, which is in Christ Jesus our Lord, nor put the believer out of reach of His call. Jesus Christ as He was going to the grave of Lazarus "wept." It shows that Jesus Christ was really and truly man, which is susceptible to the impressions of joy and grief. Jesus Christ gave this proof of His humanity, in both senses of the word that as a man, He could weep, and as merciful man, He would weep, before he gave the proof of His divinity. Tears of compassion will come to Christians, and make them resemble their Lord in merciful compassion for others.

Our Lord and Savior has given all those who believe in Him the assurances imaginable that a sincere faith shall at length be crowned with a blessed vision. If believers will take Christ's Word, and rely on His power and faithfulness, they shall see the glory of God, and be happy in His sight. If believers are to see the glory of God in their lives, they must let Christ take His own way, doing and undoing in their lives.

Jesus Christ used a very significant way of prayer because He knew that prayer is an ascent of the soul to God and the direction of its affections and emotion are Heaven ward. Christ lifted up His eyes, looking beyond the grave where Lazarus lay, and overlooked all the difficulties of this Earth. He called on God the Father with great assurance; He gave thanks to God the Father with acknowledgement of what the Father has done through Him. Believers must learn this step of prayer. We must be able to pray more and be more thankful for every prayer we raise our heart to pray to Him. We must thank God for listening to our prayers and answering our prayers at all times.

Jesus Christ our Lord and Savior here unlocked the great treasures of divine power and grace, Christ, was being assured that His prayer was answered. He gave a thankful acceptance of the answer. Believers, by faith in the promises of God, have a prospect of mercy before it is actually given. They must give thanks to God for their answered prayers. Mercies, in answer to prayer, must be done in a special manner to be acknowledged with thankfulness. Believers must know that besides the grant of mercy itself, we are to value it as a great favor to have our poor prayers being noticed by God. God answers our prayers with His infinite mercy and believers must give praise and thankfulness to God for His mercy that endures forever. Even before the Lord answer our prayers, we should give Him praise and offer thankfulness; this shows that we have strong faith in the Lord and we know that He is always there for us. He cares for His own who call unto Him with prayers and supplications.

We must thank God the Father, Son, and Holy Spirit for His cheerful guarantee of a ready answer at any time to our prayers. We must be able to depend wholly upon His ministry of intercession, and put all our petitions into His Holy hands. For we are sure that He and the Father are one and they hear our prayers always. This is the confidence we have in Him. Jesus Christ proves His mission on Earth by raising Lazarus to life.

Jesus Christ called Lazarus with a loud voice because He knew that he was too far away and was one that was dead at the same time. He exercised His power of authority over sin and death. Christ calls back the soul of Lazarus to life again; the body of Lazarus was also called from being asleep, and we usually speak loud when we awake out of sleep. This also can be viewed as the Gospel call to non-believers and people of the world, by which those who are spiritually dead were called to life by the preaching of the Gospel. It could also be seen as the triumphant at the last day with which those who are asleep in the dust shall be awakened when Christ descends and returns to Earth.

Christ called Lazarus with a loud voice, as we call those people by their name when we want to wake them from a long, fast sleep. Believers must wake up to Jesus' calling on this Earth. Believers must be able to separate themselves from the world and completely follow Christ. The power of God the Father and the power of God the Son and the Holy Spirit went along with the Word of Jesus Christ to reunite the soul and body of Lazarus, and finally Lazarus came forth and out of the grave.

This miracle of our Lord Jesus was described not by its invisible springs, to satisfy our curiosity, but by it's visible effects to confirm and strengthen our faith. Lazarus was dead four days in the tomb; our Lord Jesus Christ raised Him to life again. He called Lazarus out of the grave and gave him life everlasting.

# CHAPTER EIGHT

## PAUL & PETER RAISED THE DEAD TO LIFE

We see that Peter's in ministry; he raised Dorcas from the dead. The Scripture says: "As Peter traveled about the country, he went to visit the saints in Lydda. He healed a man that has been bedridden for 8-good years. (Aeneas, a paralytic man. From there Peter traveled to Joppa. There was a disciple named Tabitha, which when translated, is Dorcas) who was always doing good and helping the poor.

About that time she became sick and died, and her body was washed and placed in an upstairs room. Lydda was near Joppa, so when the disciples heard that Peter was in Lydda, they sent two men to him and urged him please come at once. Peter went with them and when he arrived he was taken upstairs to the room. All the widows stood around him, crying and showing him the robes and other clothing that Dorcas had made while she was still with them. Peter sent them all out of the room, and then he got down on his knees and prayed. Turning toward the dead woman, he said, 'Tabitha get up.' She opened her eyes, and seeing Peter she sat up" (Acts 9:32-40).

Our Lord said that, "I tell you the truth, anyone who has faith in me will do what I have been doing. He will do even greater things than these, because I am going to the father" (John14:12). It is our Lord's desire that the believers do the works that He did that means greater things, which included both the work of converting people to Christ and the performing of miracles. This is shown in the narratives in the Book of Acts in the Scriptures.

The reason for the greater things that believers will do is that Jesus will go to His Father and send the power of the Holy Spirit. He will also answer prayer in His Holy name, which will cover all the areas of the Gospel ministry in the entire world.

This is the reason why we see Peter kneel down and pray for a woman that had been dead for hours and she had (prepared for her funeral) and Peter with the name of Jesus Christ raised her to life again. God wanted to heal and raise Dorcas from the dead through Peter.

He also worked through Dorcas with her deeds of kindness and love. Dorcas' activity before she was sick and died did many acts of love helped those in need. This was as much as a demonstration of Christ's compassion and the Holy Spirit's presence with miracles, signs and wonders. The disciples of Jesus Christ were given assurance by the Lord that He would send a comforter, the Holy Spirit, to them, in so much that they were going to be baptized and clothed with power from above; power that will be superabundant and help them to the work of the ministry. Even up until today, without the power of the Holy Spirit, believers will not be able to live a Christian life that God requires from believers. They will not be able to witness to the sinners and the lost.

The same Lord and Savior still clothes believers with the power of the Holy Spirit up until today. There was great power from above when Peter prayed for Dorcas. The Holy Spirit prayed through him. The Spirit of the Lord used Peter's mouth to call Dorcas back to life.

This particular incidence magnifies the Holy name of our Lord Jesus Christ and His power to give life more than anything. Our Lord not only did many miracles during His earthly ministry, but he gave power of the Spirit to His disciples and many believers after the disciples, in order to effectively carry out the work of the Lord.

It is the same with Apostle Paul, "On the first day of the week we came together to break bread. Paul spoke to the people and because he intended to leave the next day, kept on talking until midnight. There were many lamps in the upstairs room where they were meeting. Seated in a window was a young man sinking into a deep sleep as Paul talked on and on. When he was sound asleep, he fell to the ground from the third story and was picked up dead. Paul went down, threw himself on the young man and put his arms around him. "Don't be alarmed," he said. "He's alive," then he went upstairs again and broke bread and ate. The people took the young man home alive and were greatly comforted" (Acts 20:7-12). The disciples came together in Troas; they read, meditated, prayed, and sang; they kept their communion with God. They then came together to worship God in music and keep up with their communion with one another.

There may be an occasion for ministers to preach not only "in season, but out of season." The preaching continued and there they set up some candles and other forms of lights. There is a young man named Eutchus in the congregation. He slept during the sermon preaching, fell down from the top and died. Believers must do everything possible to prevent sleeping during the preaching, we must get our hearts filled with the Word of God in that we hear to such a degree that we will not sleep.

God through Paul expressed great compassion and affection, as well as concern for this young man.  Paul was full of the power of the Holy Spirit.  As a sign of divine power upon the young man's dead body, Paul prayed for young man, giving life back to the young man again, which at the same time he inwardly, earnestly and in faith, he prayed.  Paul assured them that the young man has alive.  According to the Scripture, Paul returned back to his position and continued preaching.  It was a matter of great rejoicing among them, not only to the relation of the young man, but to the entire company of believers on that day.

Paul preached whatever he believed was useful or needful for the salvation of his hearers. It is the same thing today; pastors and ministers of the Gospel must be faithful to declare the whole truth of God.  They must not seek to satisfy the peoples' desires.

The day was also to celebrate the ordinance of the Lord's Supper.  In the breaking of the bread, not only the breaking of Christ's body for us, to be a sacrifice for our sins, is also commemorated, but the breaking of Christ's body to believers, which is the food and a feast for believer's souls.  Before the communion, Apostle Paul, decided to preach and as he continued preach a very long sermon; he continued until midnight because he had so many things to tell the people.

Paul preached whatever he believed was useful or needful for the salvation of his hearers. In the same way, pastors and ministers of the Gospel must be faithful to declare the whole truth of God. They must not seek to satisfy the peoples' desires or gratify their tastes, nor should they seek to promote their own selves. They must speak words of rebuke and teach the Christian doctrines that will challenge natural prejudices or preach biblical standards that oppose the desire of the sinful nature. They must also preach faithfully and deliver the whole truth and nothing but the truth.

# CHAPTER NINE

## JESUS IS THE WAY

"I am the way and the truth and the life. No one comes to the Father except through me. If you really knew me, you would know my Father as well. From now on, you do know him and have seen him" (John 14:6-7). Jesus Christ is the way to Heaven. In Him, God and man meet, and are brought together. Jesus Christ was fully human and fully divine; therefore, in Him all the fullness of God is brought together in bodily form. There is no way after the fall of Adam and Eve to get to the tree of life in the way of innocence, but Jesus Christ tells the people of His days that He is the only way.

Jesus Christ revealed this truth to His disciples and all those who followed Him during His earthly ministry. Christ tells them that if they continue following Him that they would never be out of their way, or miss the way to Heaven. Jesus Christ promisesd that the Father in Heaven will not disappoint His children. He is the only way to the Father. Christ stated that the Father loves all believing Christians more than a good earthly father loves his children, and God, the Father, wants believers to ask Him for whatever they need, promising to give us what is good.

The Son knows how greatly the Father loved us because the Father sent His only begotten Son to redeem us from our sins. Christ stated that the Father is to provide solutions for believer's problems and bread for our daily needs, but most of all, He gives the Holy Spirit to His children as their counselor and helper. Jesus Christ came to this world to save sinners. Jesus in His early teaching ministry; stated that the majority of multitudes would not follow him on the road that leads to life.

Comparatively speaking, those who enter the humble gate of true repentance and deny themselves to follow Jesus, those that sincerely endeavor to obey His command, earnestly seek His Kingdom and His righteousness, and persevere until the end of true faith, purity and love are not the many, but few. Jesus in His Sermon on the Mount describes the great blessings that will accompany discipleship in His Kingdom, but he also insists that His disciples will not escape persecution.

"Enter through the narrow gate. For wide is the gate and broad is the road that leads to destruction, and many enter through it. But small is the gate and narrow the road that leads to life, and only a few find it" (Matthew 7:13-14). Furthermore, some pastors who preach that "getting saved" is one of the easiest things in the world, are perfectly wrong. Jesus says in His Word that the thought of following Him involves many obligations concerning righteousness, acceptance of persecution, love for your enemies and self-denial and self-discipline.

Jesus Christ is the only way because the work of redemption was completed through Him. Jesus Christ is the only way because on the Cross our salvation is completed. Jesus Christ is the only way because He is the only one that came down from Heaven to save sinners of which I am one. Jesus Christ is the only way to the Father because He purchased my sins with His precious blood at Calvary. Jesus Christ is the only way to the Father because in Him all the fullness dwells. Jesus Christ is the beginning, and the middle and the end. Christ is the true living way, as well as the end of it.

Falling creation cannot come to His Father; they can only come by Christ, the Mediator of a New Covenant. Jesus Christ is the way because assurance has been built upon the Word of God, upon the sincerity of His affection to them. As He is true and would not impose upon a believer, He is kind and would not suffer them to be imposed upon. He loves believers so much and too well, to disappoint the expectations of His own people. Believers must believe and consider that the design of Jesus Christ's going back to Heaven and preparing a place for His disciples and all those that believe in Him. Christ went to prepare a place, to take possession for all believers as our advocate, to secure our title as indefeasible; to make provision for the happiness of Heaven, which must be lifted up from humanity.

Heaven consists of the presence of Christ; it was therefore, designed to prepare us for eternal life in Him. Many people go to church every Sunday, but they did not know Christ. They know Him and yet did not know Him as well as they might and should have known Him. Jesus Christ is the way to Heaven. Believe in Him you have eternal life.

# CHAPTER TEN

## JESUS CHRIST IS THE TRUTH

"In the beginning was the Word, and the Word was with God, and the Word was God. He was with God in the beginning" (John 1:1). Apostle John begins his gospel by clear explanation that Christ is the Word, in using this designated name for Christ, John presented Christ to the people of this world as the personal Word of God, as well as indicating that in these last days, God has been spoken through His Son to all the believers and non-believers. Scripture declares that Jesus Christ is the manifold wisdom of God and the power of God. Christ is the perfect revelation of the nature and the person of God. It is just as individual people's words reveal his or her heart and mind.

Christ as the Word of God reveals the heart and mind of the Father. God gave us three different characteristics of Jesus Christ as the Word. The Word in relation to the Father, Christ was pre-existent with God the Father before the creation of the world. He was a person existing from eternity, distinct from, but in eternal fellowship with God the Father. Christ was the divine Word of God and was God, having the same nature and essence as the Father. Jesus Christ is the Word in relation to the world. It was through Jesus Christ that God the Father created and continues to sustain the universe.

The Word in relation to all humanity, the Word became flesh. The Son of God took on human nature, but without sin. This is the basic statement of truth of the incarnation; Jesus Christ left Heaven and entered the condition of human life through the gateway of human birth and became the God man. Jesus Christ was not created; He is eternal and He has always been in loving fellowship with God the Father and the Holy Spirit.

Jesus Christ is the true light and genuine life is embodied in Christ Jesus. His life was light for everyone. Jesus Christ is God's truth; nature and power that is made available to all people that came to the world through Him. "For the law was given through Moses, grace and truth came through Jesus Christ. No one has ever seen God, but God, the one and only who is at the Father's side, has made him known" (John 1:17-18).

Grace and truth came through Jesus Christ because those who were under the Old Testament Covenant there was a measure of grace as seen in the faith of few people. "The Lord then said to Noah; Go into the Ark, you and your whole family, because I have found you righteous in this generation" (Genesis 7:1). And in the promises of forgiveness, "Abraham believed the Lord, and he credited it to him as righteousness" (Genesis 15:6). The Scripture mentioned faith and righteousness together in the Old Testament. Faith, trust and reliance on God; this means that believers must persevere in trust and belief by manifesting obedience and faithfulness.

This was what Abraham possessed; his heart was turned towards God in an enduring trust, obedience and submission. God saw Abraham's heart – attitude of faith and credited it to him as righteousness, which means being in the right relationship with God and with His will. Now through Jesus Christ, grace and truth are available to the fullest extent. Truth is no longer veiled through the types such as sacrifices.

There is always one blessing after another means there is a constant impartation of grace and power that is given to believers who respond to the grace given them. Grace is God's initiative, love and favor that make it possible for believer's salvation in Christ as they receive Him. Salvation does not come by any efforts of believers to keep the law, but by the Holy Spirit and Jesus Christ's grace coming into believers lives to regenerate believer's spirits and recreate believers in a Christ like image. Jesus Christ is the truth. In Him humanity and deity where united together in Him. In a humble submission was given a way to the Father. He entered life with all the limitations of human experiences.

Jesus Christ is the truth because he is the Lamb of God provided by God to be sacrifice in the place of sinners, by His death, Jesus provided for the removal of the guilt and power of sin and He opened the way to God for all people in the world. "Sanctify them by the truth; your word is truth" (John 17:17). Our Lord prayed for the disciples during His priestly prayer before His crucifixion. He prays that the Father sanctify the disciples and those who will believe Him through them. The Word sanctify means to make them holy, or to separate, set them apart for the work God the Father assigned them to do.

On the evening, before our Lord's crucifixion, Jesus prays that His disciples would be a holy people, separated from the world and sin for the purpose of worshiping and serving the Lord God. Jesus prays that they must be set apart in order to get close to God, to live for Him and to be like Him.

This sanctification can only be accomplished by believers' devotion to the truth revealed to them by the Holy Spirit, the Spirit of truth.  The truth is both the living Word of God and the revelation of God's written Word.

# CHAPTER ELEVEN

## JESUS CHRIST IS THE LIFE

Jesus Christ is the life; in Him there is life everlasting. "For God so loved the world that he gave his one and only Son, that whoever believes in him shall not perish but have eternal life" (John 3:16). This Scripture reveals the heart and purpose of God for humanity. God's love is so large and wide enough to embrace all the people on Earth. God the Father gave His Son as an offering for our past present and future sins on the Cross at Calvary. Christ's atonement proceeds from the loving heart of God. It was something that God planned before the foundation of the universe.

"He who did not spare his own Son, but gave him up for us all how will he not also, along with him, graciously give us all things?" (Romans 8:32). God's plan and purpose is love and to redeem humanity through Jesus Christ. The recipient of God's foreknowledge is stated in the plural, refers to the believers the church of Jesus Christ on Earth.  God in His infinite mercy loved humanity even when we were in sin and trespasses.

God's love is primarily for the Body of Christ and it includes the individuals only as they identify themselves with His body through abiding faith in and through union with Jesus Christ.  The Body of Christ will attain to glorification, although, individual believers will fall short of such glorification if they separate themselves from the love of God and fail to maintain their faith in Christ.

God the Father is the one that always made the believers alive in Jesus Christ through the power of the Holy Spirit.  Jesus Christ is the giver of life.  "This is love; not that we loved God, but that he loved us and sent his Son as an atoning sacrifice for our sins" (1$^{st}$ John 4:10).  We share Christ's nature because we are born of Him.  God loved us, we who have experience His love, His forgiveness and help are obligated to help others even at great personal cost.

If we love one another, God will continue to make us alive and live in us and His love is made perfect and complete in all believers. Believers will continue to live in the life of Jesus Christ if they remain in Christ, have fellowship with the Father and sincerely endeavor to obey

His commands. Believers must continue to separate from the world, remain in the truth of God's Word and love others, then they will have confidence that His life and love are in us and we will not be condemned on the Day of Judgment.

In order to remain in the life of Christ, believers must have a genuine love and faith that will express great gratitude to the love of God, the Father and God, the Son. Faith in God and love for God are inseparable, for when we are born of God, the Holy Spirit pours the love of God in Christ Jesus into our hearts. A total surrender to Christ's Lordship for believers requires three important elements. One: conviction that Jesus Christ is the true Son of God and the only Savior for the lost humanity. Two: self-surrendering fellowship with obedience to Christ. "I am the true vine, and my Father is the Gardner. He cuts off every branch in me that bears no fruit, while every branch that does bear fruit he prunes so that it will be even more fruitful" (John 15:1-2). Our Lord and Savior describes Himself as the true vine, which means those who put their faith in Christ and have become His disciples are like branches which receive life from the vine. Three: By remaining attached to Jesus Christ as the source of our life, believers will able to produce fruit for the Kingdom. God is the Gardner who takes care of the branches means that the believers and those who are still going to believe in Christ; in order that they may bear more fruit, God expects all the believers of Jesus Christ to bear more and more fruit.

Jesus Christ came to the world to save sinners. The offer that is made of salvation by Jesus Christ is for all people in the world. The salvation offered is complete; they shall never perish. This is the great Gospel mystery that revealed Jesus Christ as the only begotten Son of God. Now you know that God the Father loves us because He gave us His only begotten Son. It pleased God gave His Son; God gave Him up to suffer and die for our sin.

Herein God has commended His love to the world. It is a wonder that a Holy God should love the people in the world. Christ tells the Jews that He came in love to the whole world, to save the Gentiles, as well as the Jews. Through Jesus Christ there is a general offer of life and salvation. The greatest benefit is that whoever believes in Christ shall not perish because God has taken away their past, present and future sin, they shall not die: Christ has purchased the believers pardon on the Cross. Believers are entitled to the joy of Heaven. They shall have everlasting life that only in Him the world might be saved. God the

Father was in God the Son reconciling the whole world to Him without imputing their sins.

75

# CHAPTER TWELVE

## JESUS CHRIST IS THE SOURCE OF LIFE WITH GOD

Eternal life is the gift that God the Father bestowed on all the believers of Jesus Christ when they are born again. Eternal life, life in Jesus Christ is where believers live forever, not only expresses perpetuity, but also it is a quality of life from this Earth to Heaven. It is a divine type of life, a life that frees believers from the power of sin and Satan, death, and removes believers from what is merely earthly in order to know God and the power of His resurrection.

The New Testament Scripture clearly teaches that the Lord Jesus Christ Himself breaks the power and the dominion of sin in the lives of those who are true Christ followers. Individuals who habitually sin are still slaves to sin and unrighteousness and therefore, they are the children of the devil.

The union of sincere believers with Christ in His death and resurrection will result in freedom from sin's power and dominion. The context of human reasoning and knowledge determine that many things are true. Yet, there is only one truth that will set the people of this world free from sin; it is clearly the destruction of Satan's dominion.

Jesus Christ Himself and His revelation of truth in the Scripture offers believers the sanctifying power of His life because He is the life, whereby, we who follow the spirit are set free from the desires of the sinful nature, and believers are able to live a holy life.

"For the grace of God that brings salvation has appeared to all men. It teaches us to say no to ungodliness and worldly passions, and to live with self-control, upright and godly lives in this present age" (Titus 2:11-12). The grace of God describes the character and purpose of God's saving grace. According to Apostle Paul, saving grace has appeared to all the people everywhere in the world, not just to a selected people who are the elect from eternity. Believers must reject ungodly passions, pleasures and values of the present age and regard them as abominable. Jesus Christ commands believers and empowers believers to live upright and godly lives.

While waiting for the return of our Lord and Savior Jesus Christ in His appearing, Jesus Christ is our hope of glory. Christ Jesus is the life of every believer; without Him we are nothing. Christ is the life, the true life of God the Father and God the Son. Jesus Christ is our blessed hope, and our hope of glory. Blessed hopes implies that a fullness of blessings, as well as God's gracious favor and happiness of being in the new bodies that will be made alive in Christ that will be immortal and not subjected to corruption or decay.

This is believer's great hope, which relates to the glorious appearing of the Lord Jesus Christ and it will occur when Christ comes for His bride, the blood washed church. We are to wait for this great moment prayerfully, in faith and purity and with fervent desire as a faithful and chaste bride. Jesus Christ is the hope of all who believe in Him. We wait patiently for Your glorious return which nobody knows the hour, or the time, but the Scripture said, it will happen at the twinkling of an eye, the trumpet will sound and all who believe in Him will be alive in Him and forever live with the Lord. Jesus Christ is the life of all the people in the world.

# CHAPTER THIRTEEN

## JESUS CAME TO EARTH TO GIVE LIFE

"The thief comes only to steal and kill and destroy, I have come that they may have life and have it to the full. I am the good shepherd. The good shepherd lays down his life for the sheep" (John 10: 10-11). Those who believe in Jesus Christ will be saved. They will have abundant life that only Christ gives. Believers will have all that they need to be delivered from sin, guilt and condemnation. Jesus Christ is the giver of life; the only gate for salvation, there is none other. "Salvation is found in no one else, for there is no other name under heaven given to man by which we must be saved (Acts 4:12).

The disciples were convinced that the greatest need of every individual was salvation from sin and the wrath of God, and they preached that this need could be met by no one else, other than Jesus Christ. This truth reveals the exclusive nature of the Gospel and the churches' heavy responsibility of preaching the Gospel to every person. If there were other ways of salvation, the church could be at ease. According to the teaching of our Lord and Savior during His earthly ministries, there is no hope for anyone apart from salvation through Him.

Jesus Christ is the giver of spiritual life; it is spiritual dynamics that work behind the scenes of human activity in the world. Satan was clearly named the one who is the "thief," whose primary mission is to steal, kill and destroy people's lives, health, families, purpose in life and everything that is good. Jesus has come to counter and destroy Satan's evil work by the power of the Cross and by giving life that is redemptive and full to those who believe in Him and receive Him as Lord and Savior.

No one can know and experience the fullness of the life that Jesus gives apart from Jesus and the indwelling presence of His life giving Holy Spirit. Jesus Christ declares Himself to be the promised Good Shepherd. Jesus was tender in mercy and He cares for all the people in the world, especially those who believe in Him.

Jesus Christ is the door of the sheep; we must come in by Him as the door. Believers must, by faith, come into covenant and communion with Christ.

True believers are in the good hands of Christ; when they go out, they are kept safe from wolves, as well as they will have the liberty to come again when they come in. They are not shut in as trespassers, but they have liberty to go out and come in they are always safe at the pasture.

Christ said, "I have come so that they can have life, life abundant." Abundant life means the fullness of life of believers, it also refers to the expectations of prosperity and good health and can also include all other forms of fullness of life in Christ, which begins with new birth, new relationships, new relationships with fellow human beings and fellow believers engaging in spiritual maturity that will help believers to continue living an abundant life, having been cleansed from sin and sin nature.

Abundant life is not a movement or a unique doctrine, but a name that applied to the teachings and expectations of believers or all the people groups in the world. It is a form of fullness of life that can face any diverse circumstance or trouble. The abundant life that Jesus Christ offered it is the abounding fullness of joy and strength in mind, spirit, body and soul.

It signifies a contrast to feelings of lack, emptiness, dissatisfaction and many other unforeseen circumstances that can motivate a believer or non-believer who are seeking to find meaning to their life by so doing in their life to bring a change for the better.

The abundant life shows that God is good and His goodness endures forever.  He always wants to bless His children spiritually, physically and economically.  The abundant life of a believer begins from new birth, and a new relationship with God Almighty.  God always wants to maintain good relationship with all the people on Earth. Believers must be learning how to live the abundant life, completely clean from sin, pray without ceasing to fight a spiritual battle in this world.

Focus on the Lord at all times and do what is pleasing in His sight.  Salvation is an essential element of abundant life.  A believer's life in Jesus Christ consists of complete trust and obedience in Him, accompanied by strong faith in Him, with evangelism and outreach that fights poverty, disease, hunger, injustice, and ignorance this is evidence of their faith in Him.  The Scripture says, "Every good and perfect gift is from above, coming down from the Father of the heavenly lights, who does not change like shifting shadows.  He chose to give us birth through the word of truth, that we might be a kind of first fruits of all he created" (James 1:17).

God's Word warns all the believers that they should let no one deceive them with empty words, because of such things God's wrath comes; therefore, do not be partners with any evil things. We as believers must take righteousness and holy living seriously. Our houses must be swept clean and filled with God's Word, as well as the holiness of Christ.

A believer's new life in Christ begins when they were born again, through the Word of truth in Christ. The new life that Jesus Christ is telling us, so get rid of all moral filth that offends and grieves the Holy Spirit, so that we will be steadfast in accepting God's Word into our mind, heart, spirit, soul, and body. Jesus Christ came to put life into the flock, the church in general which had seemed rather like a valley full of dry bones and thin like a pasture covered over with flocks. He came to give life to those who believe in Him, not just anybody, but to a particular people who trust Him and made Him their Lord and Savior.

He came to give them abundant life. A life with all inclusive of all good that they might have it more abundantly than they could have expected or more than what they ask for in prayer or more that they could imagine. Christ is the giver of life. He came to give life and much, much more, abundantly and offers something better than anything in this world. Life in Christ is immeasurable and full of joy that money cannot buy.

## CHAPTER FOURTEEN

## BELIEVE IN HIM AND YOU WILL LIVE FOREVER

"And whoever lives and believes in me will never die. Do you believe this?" (John 11:26). Christ is telling us again and again that in Him there is life and life everlasting. For the believers who believes in Jesus, physical death is not an end, instead it a gateway to an abundant eternal life. "The blood of Jesus! Sin dies in its presence, death ceases to be death: heaven's gates are opened. The blood of Jesus we shall march on conquering to conquer, so long as we trust its power" (Charles Spurgeon 1884).

We have seen from the beginning how God exercised authority over human kind right from the Garden of Eden with Adam and Eve. The Scripture reveals to us clearly the authority of God over man, as a created being with reasoning and freedom of free will.

The Lord God Almighty commanded the man, who stood as the Father and the representative of all mankind to receive the Law, as he had lastly received a nature. Man was created to be capable of performing reasonable services and therefore, he received not only the command of a creation, but the command as a prince and as a master.

God confirmed that Adam and Eve's secret of their happiness was granted by God, but of every tree in the Garden they can eat, but this is a sign of liberty and love of God to them. It was an assurance of life to Him, immortal life, upon His obedience and upon condition of perfect personal and perpetual obedience. Adam and Eve were assured to live in Paradise with Him, as well as their descendants forever.

A trial of his obedience forfeited all his happiness. Adam's nature was an aversion to that which was evil, only because it was forbidden. This restraint was laid upon his desires of flesh and of the mind, which, is in the corrupt nature of man, are the two great fountains of sin. The tree of life, which was intended to make physical death impossible, is related to eternal life endless life.

As long as Adam and Eve believed God's Word and obeyed, he would continue to live in eternal life and in blessed fellowship with God. It is the same today as long as we live in Christ, we will continue in new life in Him. In the Scripture our Lord and Savior said, "I am the resurrection and the life"(John 11:25). Jesus Christ made it clear that for everyone on this Earth who believes in Jesus, physical death is not a tragic end. It is instead the way to the life in Christ where all believers will have an intimate relationship with God the Father, Son and Holy Spirit forever.

The Word of God is God; the Word of God will never die as long as believers follow Christ by faith and not by sight. The power of Jesus Christ's death is incomparable and incomprehensible. Jesus Christ told Martha, "I am the resurrection and the Life." There is no other way, and nobody else can do it, the life eternal is only in Jesus Christ. It is the endless life; a life everlasting that can only be found in the person of Jesus Christ.

This is a great word of encouragement from our Lord, even to us today. It is a great word of comfort to know that whatever we are going through on this Earth, we have Jesus Christ who is our hope of glory. We know that in Him, there is everlasting life. We know that the power of Christ is His sovereign power. Jesus Christ is our great intercessor. Believers must know that when Christ prays, God will give anything He asks for, but He will let us also know that by His Word He can do everything and by His Word Heaven was made.

This is an unspeakable comfort to all believers of Jesus Christ. Christ's life is our life and Christ lives in us and we live in Christ. The promise of life that believers will never die is to those who believe in Him. Believer's bodies will be resurrected and, "Whoever lives and believes in me will never die. Do you believe this" (John 11:26)? Jesus Christ expressed His promise to Martha who clearly understood Christ was referring to all the inhabitants of the world who will believe in Him, whether Jewish or Gentile. We will live with Him forever. Resurrection is a return to life where Christ Jesus is the author of that return and that life to which we return. Believers return to Him and live with Him forever. Our Lord said he or she that believes in Him by faith is born again to a heavenly and divine life. The body of the believer was promised a blessed immortality.

And he that lives and believes shall never die. The spiritual life shall never be extinguished, but perfected for eternal life, life everlasting. The life of the soul shall be immediately at death swallowed up into immortality. Though the body is dead because of sin, but yet the soul shall live forever because of Christ Jesus' righteousness.

Jesus Christ said, "I am the living bread; I am the living bread that came down from heaven. If anyone eats of this bread, he will live forever. This bread is my flesh, which I will give for the life of the world" (John 6:51). We must receive spiritual life by believing in Christ and sharing in His redemptive benefits of His death on the Cross. Jesus Christ is the living Word; the Bible is the written Word of God. Jesus calls Himself here the Bread of Life.

Jesus Christ relates this bread to the Word of God. He said in another Scripture that, "Man must not live on bread alone, but on every Word that comes out of the mouth of God" (Matthew 4:4).

God knows what is good for all the believers. God shall order for His children anything that is always good. Anything that God shall appoint for our end, will be as good, as a livelihood for man as bread and it will maintain him, as well as, in that we believers might eat the earthly bread and yet the earthly bread does not nourish us. It is the same if we deny God His blessing of the Bread of Life.

It is God's blessings that make believers to yearn for the abundant Bread of Life, which we cannot live without. Believers must learn how to live for God and do everything in His Holy name. "That everyone who believes in him may have eternal life" (John3:15). Here is the great Gospel benefit that whoever believes in Christ shall not die. God has taken away their sin, they shall not die; a pardon has been purchased through the precious blood atonement of Jesus Christ. Believers are entitled to the joys of Heaven; they shall also have everlasting life.

# CHAPTER FIFTEEN

## AWARENESS OF GOD IN OUR LIVES

God the Father Almighty, the compassionate and gracious God, all powerful, all knowing, all merciful and mighty, who is full of truth and righteousness, abounding in loving kindness, mercy and love. Our God has compute knowledge of everyone on the universe. All our thoughts and our actions are naked, open before Him. It is always good and rewarding to meditate on God's divine truths and will for our lives, thereby we shall live by applying these truths to ourselves in all the areas of our lives.

Believers should learn and practice how to lift their heart up in prayer to the Lord, instead of occupying their minds with unprofitable, unfriendly and unloving things. As we know that God is the all-knowing of all things; He is the omniscient, which means that He is everywhere every time. He is the omnipresent. His truths must be acknowledged by all the people in the world. God who takes notice of every step we make, every right or wrong steps we take, is the ruler of souls of all human beings. He knows which step and walk we walk, either towards Him or far away from Him.

God knows when we move away from Him and follow or keep bad company. He knows what is in every human heart, either we belong to Him or we belong to many ritual things of this world. There is not a word that we spoke that He does not know how the thought came to us and with what way we uttered it out.

Wherever we are, whatever we are doing, we are under the love and controlling eye and hand of God. We cannot know how God searches or by what means He sees us. Wherever we may be, we are in His Garden; if we who believe in Him should think about this, as well as those who say there is no God, they will stay away from evil and think no evil against each other.

People of this world should know that someone is watching over them every step of the way. As long as we are still in this tent, which means this body that our soul lives in, we cannot see God, but God sees us perfectly every time. There is nothing, nothing that can hide us from the Almighty God - no clothing, no darkness; there is no any form of disguise that can hide us from God. He is the creator of Heaven and Earth. Everything that He created obeys Him and He purposes them as instrument to carry out His purposes.

The light cannot hide us. He sees through the greatest light; He created the light. We believers must be very happy and rejoice because nothing can remove us from the sustaining hand of God and comforting presence of the Almighty God. Even if believers are persecuted or killed, his soul will ascend to Heaven and live with Christ forever.

Nothing can separate him or her from the love of Jesus Christ, the Savior, who will raise the persecuted Christian's body to a glorious body. Nothing can separate believers from their Lord. Believers are always happy doing the service of the Lord by exercising strong faith, hope and with prayers. Jesus Christ is the Rock of salvation of those who believe in Him.

Hallelujah, because of Him and through Him, and to Him are all things that pertain to this world and knowledge: comfort, health, safety, progress, power and usefulness.

Let all His creation bless His Holy Name. Our primary goal on this Earth is to bless the Lord. The earth is full of His praises and thankfulness. The sand at the seashore, the flowers, the insects, animals, birds of the air, mountains, rivers, trees clouds, the sun, moon and stars, all the Nine other Planets from this Earth to Pluto, all must give His praises that are due to Him.

All the people of this Earth, young and old, children, babies, household pets must give unceasing praises to God. All the servants of God, all the people of God, must give Him praises that are due Him. All places of His dominion must praise His Holy Name. Everything on Earth and under the Earth must praise His Holy Name. Let all the ministers, pastors, reverends and ordain ministers preach and teach the true Gospel that will make the heart of people open and give themselves to the Almighty God.

Let them seek, knock, ask and pray to God in spirit and in truth forever and forever. The Spirit says, "Come Lord Jesus."

# CHAPTER SIXTEEN

## WHY WE MUST BELIEVE

We must believe because Jesus Christ is the only begotten Son of God. Christ is the Word incarnate; He is the Alpha and the Omega, the beginning and the end, the first and the last. He is the God of resurrection, eternal who has immortality in the light. He came to this world to save sinners and the people of this world from all their sin.

He came for all the people in the world who will believe in Him. Christ, as the Word of God, became flesh and dwelt among us. We beheld His glory, the glory of the one and only true Son of God, full of grace and truth. We must believe in the everlasting life that Jesus Christ offers because He is the bread of life. He is the Bread that if anyone eats of Him, he shall never die.

He is the water of life, a living water, a spiritual water, the water that if you drink you will never thirst; the water will be a spring of water welling up to eternal life.

Jesus Christ told Nicodemus, "You must be born again," because if you believe in Jesus Christ He will make you a new creature, old things pass away and behold all things become new. Believers have a new life in Christ, a new nature and a new way of living on this Earth. Jesus Christ is the Door that you trust. In Him you will freely go to and fro and find pasture. Christ is the Door of the sheep; the sheep knows the Shepherd, and the Shepherd knows the sheep. We must believe because the love of God in Christ Jesus cannot be compared will any love on Earth.

We believe because Jesus Christ was crucified, was dead and buried and rose again for our justification. He paid my pardon and your pardon on the Cross. He ascended to Heaven and seated at the right hand of God. He will be coming back quickly to judge the dead and all eyes shall see Him.

We must believe because He is the only one, the giver of life. He is life; believe in Him you will live forever. Jesus Christ is the only one with an empty tomb. Believe in Him and you will have life that is a life to the fullest. His empty tomb is our empty tomb; His resurrection is our resurrection. All believers automatically resurrected with Christ.

Why we should believe because in Christ God gave believers the gift of the indwelling of the Holy Spirit. The Spirit of Jesus Christ indwells and lives in believers forever, controlling, directing, instructing, teaching, helping, guiding and living the life of Jesus Christ in the believer.

Believers of Jesus Christ rest from all their works and rest on the Lord. Jesus Christ is the giver of life. Believes in Him and you will have life in Him.

We must believe in Christ's love to all who believe in Him is a genuine love, abiding love of the Father and Son, master and friend, the Holy Spirit. Christ's love is an irreversible love for those who gave their life to Him. This is why should we believe Jesus Christ is the one that has regeneration power to those who repent of their sins and turn to God, and put their faith in the Lord Jesus Christ alone for salvation alone.

Regeneration involves a transition from the old sin nature of life, of sin to a new life of faithful loving obedience to Jesus Christ. Believers make every decision with the power of God and Jesus Christ, where those who are truly born again, are set free from their sins.

Why we should believe because the Scripture says, "For God so loved the world that he gave his one and only Son that whoever believers in him shall not perish but have eternal life" (John3:16).   God reveals the heart and the purpose of God.   God's love is so amazing that it embraces all the people on Earth.   God gave His only Son as a sin offering on the Cross; on the Cross, our salvation was completed.

We should believe because Jesus Christ is the God of light; in Him there is no darkness.   He moves those who believe in Him from the domain of darkness to His glorious and everlasting light.   This is the true light that shines and no darkness can comprehend it.   Jesus Christ's light shined on the believer the very moment of conversion.   Jesus Christ is the pure light of the world.   Christ gave light to the baby in the womb before they arrived on this Earth, so when they arrive, they will just continue in the light of God living their life for Jesus Christ from the beginning of their life to the end.

We must believe because we do not want to be condemned with the world.   People of the world do not want to agree with God's future accountability and the judgment concerning their sins in repentance and salvation.

We should believe in Jesus Christ because He is the only one that grace and truth are available to the extent of one blessing after other blessing in a constant impartation of grace and power for believers who respond to the grace bestowed upon them.

# SUMMARY

From the beginning of creation, the life of God is a life of blessings and power and love. Jesus Christ is the friend of the sinners. Obedience that is commanded from the Old Testament to the New Testament is still very important, even in our modern world.

Christ said, "For God did not send his Son into the world to condemn the world, but to save the world through him"(John 3:17). Jesus Christ is the eternal Word of God, believe in Him and you have life and life everlasting. Jesus Christ commanded all the believers to love in a greater and special way to love one another. Believers must distinguish the truth from those whose profession is false by examining their love for the obedience to Jesus Christ and their loyalty to God's Holy Word.

Jesus Christ belongs to all the people in the world; whoever possess a living faith in Him and remains faithful to His command, and to God's Holy Word and sincerely understands the Word of God, Christ is one in him and that believer deserves special love and support from the Holy Spirit in everything they do and anywhere they are in this world.

If we love the Lord Jesus with our whole heart, mind, spirit, soul, body, we must love all true believers around the world. As believers, we must never compromise God's holiness or love for God. His will as revealed in His Word must control our love for others, especially non-believers that we will make all efforts to introduce them to Christ. Believers must try their best to make sure the sinners will taste the Lord and see how good He is in the life of every believer.

Believing and surrendering your life to Him, you will never die. Jesus Christ has the power to save to the outermost those who come to Him. Jesus Christ asked the Father to give the Holy Spirit to those who are serious about their love for Him, and their devotion to His Word. Jesus Christ emphasized that believers should continue in their attitude of love and obedience to Him.

"The World and its desires pass away but the man who does the will of God lives forever" (1st John 2:17). Believer are crucified to the world, their love should be reserved and based on God. Believers must throw out all the worldly lust that it is not ordained of God. The things of the world are distinguished into three classes according to the Scriptures: There is the lust of the flesh (buying all sorts of luxury material things in the world).  There is the lust of the eyes: this is ambitions, selfish-ambitions that must be abandoned and renounced.  The love of appetite or the pride of life: this is a desire for all selfish ambitions that must be mortified and denounced.  They are vain and earthly in the state of those things of the world that are fading away.

The immortality of the love of God, the object of His love in opposition to the world that passed away abides forever.  Love shall never fail.  The love of God must be continuously be growing in the life of all the believers of Jesus Christ.

## GOD'S LOVING KINDNESS

God always give wealth, knowledge and wisdom to an individual with whom He wants them to share and He wants it to flow to others as a river or an ocean. He gave individuals great wisdom in so many areas of life such as wisdom and knowledge of engineering, technological innovations, medical breakthroughs with regards to so many diseases that plague people in the world. For example, the HIV medicine, the knowledge of teaching, hearing aids, eye transplants, kidney transplants and heart transplants, just to name a few.

He bestowed His favor upon Moses by answering Moses' prayer. He agreed to go with Moses and the people. All God's children should fervently pray, offer ceaseless prayers to know His ways, His heart, purpose, wisdom, holy knowledge, principles and even His suffering where we come to know God. God answered Moses' prayer because He respected him. He considered him as a friend, and He was pleased with him. Moses found favor because even though the people of Israel disobeyed God. Moses remained loyal and faithful to the Lord and mediated between the Lord and the people of Israel.

God changed King Saul's inner disposition through His anointing by the Holy Spirit.  This change was unconditional or permanent, but something that could be maintained only by the Holy fellowship with a loving obedience to God.  God's anointed King is Jesus, the Messiah, the Anointed One, whom God anointed with the Holy Spirit.  All believers of Jesus Christ must be anointed with the same Holy Spirit as New Covenant priests and kings.

"While they were there, the time came for her to deliver her child.  And she gave birth to her firstborn son and wrapped him in bands of cloth, and laid him in a manger, because there was no place for them in the inn.  In that region there were shepherds living in the fields, keeping watch over their flock by night.  Then an angel of the Lord stood before them and the glory of the Lord shone around them, and they were terrified.  But the angel said to them, 'Do not be afraid, for see I am bringing you good news of great joy for all the people.  To you is born this day in the city of David a Savior, who is the Messiah, the Lord'" (Luke2:6-11).  Christ the Lord has been anointed as the Messiah of God and the Lord who rules over His people.

Our actions toward those who are unkind to us, such as the bully kids intentionally looking for some good kids to beat up in schools or in the neighborhood, should be such that it might lead them to accept Christ as their Savior. Jesus Christ shows us this example when He was on the Cross.  He prayed for His persecutors.  Stephen was one of the first converted Christians when he was martyred, put Jesus' command into practice as he prayed for those who were stoning him before he died.

## BIOBLIOGRAPHY


Dana, H. E., <u>Searching the Scriptures</u>, Kansas City Central Seminary Press (1946).

Donald P Husted, <u>The Worshiping Church Hynarale,</u> Hope Publishing (190).

Fission, Floyd, <u>Origin of the Gospel</u>, New York, Abingdon Press (1938).

Goodspeed, Edger J., <u>An Introduction to New Testament</u>, Chicago University of Chicago Press (1937).

Hayes D. A., <u>The Septic Gospel and Acts,</u> New York: Methodist Book Concern, (1919). (The Best Introduction to these four books of New Testament).

Hurter, A.M.A., <u>Pattern For Life</u>, Philadelphia, Westminster Press, (1953).

James D. Smart, <u>The Interpretation of Scripture</u>, The Westminster Press Philadelphia USA (1961).

Morgan G. Campbell, <u>The Parables of the Kingdom</u>, New York, Fleming H. Revell Company (1907).

Philip Yancey and Tim Stafford, <u>The Student Bible New Revised Standard Version</u>, Zondervan, Grand Rapids, Michigan USA (1994).

Ralph Earle, <u>Exploring New Testament</u>, Beacon Hill Press (1955).

Reo. Leslie, <u>Matthew Henry Commentary in one Volume</u> Zondervan Publishing House (1960).

<u>Student Study Bible NRSV</u>, Zondervan, Grand Rapids, Michigan USA (1994).

Walter, <u>Evangelical Dictionary of Biblical Theology</u> by Vlwell Baker Books, Grand Rapids, Michigan (1973).

William MacDonald Edited by Art Farstad, <u>Believer's Bible Commentary</u>, Thomas Nelson Publishers, Nashville, Atlanta (1995) and (1972) Edition Vancouver, London.

## BIBLICAL INDEX

Acts 9:33-40, 20:7-12, 9:36-43, 26:8, 20:7-12, 16:32

Romans  8:1-20,  3:23,  6:23,  1:18-23,  8:32,  12:12,  10:14, 2:7,5:8, 10:9-10,

1st Corinthians 15:42-55

2nd Corinthians 5:17

Galatians 5:20-22, 3, 1-20

Ephesians2:1, 4:20-24, 2:2-10,3:20-21, 2:6-8, 3:8,

Philippians 3:10

Colossians 1:15-16

1st Thessalonians 4:13, 5:224:16-17,

2nd Thessalonians 1:5,

Titus 2:11-12

1st Timothy 6:23, 1:16

Hebrews 2:3, 1:13, 12, 39, 7:25

James 2:12-22,

1st Peter 8: 2, 5:10,

2nd Peter1:16

1st John 2:17, 2:25

Jude  1-25

Revelation 3:7, 1:18

Books previously Published by the author:
**Grace Dola Balogun**
by
Grace Religious Books Publishing & Distributors, Inc.
New York

## PRAYER THE SOURCE OF STRENGTH FOR LIFE -
### English Edition

*Prayer the Source of Strength for Life* is a powerful book that will energize your spirit to pray more and more until the prayer is part of your life and until the gate of Heaven is opened and your prayer is answered. Your prayer life will change your life.

**LA ORACION FUENTE DE FORTALEZA PARA LA VIDA – Spanish Edition.**

Dios no's dio el poder de la oracion, quiere que lo usemos; debemos illamar, comunicarnos con el en todo lo que estemo spasando. El espera saber denosotros.

## Spirit Power Volumes I and II

*Spirit Power Volumes I and II* both discuss the power of the Holy Spirit in the lives of believers.

The Power of the Spirit of God begins from the creation of the world up until today. That power will also continue until Christ returns to reign. Hallelujah

## THE CROSS AND THE CRUCIFIXION

Our Lord Jesus Christ died on the Cross to bring forth love and compassion. Sin's impact on human life brings all other evil into our world, from one society to another society, from one culture to another.

But in Christ, we are clothed with His holiness. We have the gift of eternal life. The gate of Heaven is open and we are eligible for our inheritance in Heaven.

Hallelujah! Hosanna in the Highest. Jesus Christ paid it all, unto Him all we owe. The Cross of Christ is the Cross of joy, peace, and righteousness to all who believe in Him.

**Three Simple Solutions for World Peace**

*Three Simple Solutions for World Peace* is a book that clears all the confusion that many people of the world have been going through for many years. It is a book that gives light and advice to some of the problems that plague the world, and that offers solutions for these problems. It is a book that is full of knowledge, understanding and solutions that will bring some peace to the world.

**Justification by Faith Alone in Christ Alone**

*Justification by Faith Alone in Christ Alone* will clear all the confusion of believers' faith in Jesus Christ. Believers will also rejoice in the long sufferings – they will rejoice in their sufferings, afflictions, persecutions, rejections and all various trials that may press in on them because these long sufferings will help all the believers to be redeemed in Christ.

## CHRISTIAN CELL PHONE SERIES:

***Christian Cell Phone Godly Wisdom*** helps readers understand the role of God's wisdom and the importance of obtaining godly wisdom in one's life to produce prosperous results in all areas of life. These areas are critical and include family, relationships and finances. The acquiring of God's wisdom is to be sought after in life and will impact others as well.

***Christian Cell Phone God's Favor*** is designed to give readers knowledge of God's favor from the Old Testament to the New Testament. With an analysis of the favor that was on Jesus, the Son of God, the reader will find that God's favor can completely change one's life and lead others to Christ as well.

***Christian Cell Phone God's Anointing*** takes a look at the anointing on the life of Jesus that includes present day believers in Christ Jesus. This anointing can be applied to all areas of life and can be seen in miraculous ways. The anointing is what makes our life incredible and supernatural, drawing all those who see, to Christ.

## JESUS CHRIST THE JOY OF CHRISTMAS

*Jesus Christ the Joy of Christmas* gives praise and tribute to the child that was born in Bethlehem. Tracing the prophecies of Old about this King that was born, the author gives an account of the sinless Lamb of God who came to take away the peoples' sin from a biblical perspective, who is the real Joy of Christmas.

## PRAYER FOR THE BULLY VICTIMS AND THE BULLY TOO!

*Prayer for the Bully Victims and the Bully Too* addresses the issue of the bully from the classroom to the home. By the use of scriptural application, the author takes a look at what can be done to help the bully kid and their victims. The author has written several key prayers that readers can use to help either the bully victim or parents who are dealing with a child that has become a bully.

## I AM THE RESURRECTION AND THE LIFE

*I Am The Resurrection and The Life:* Powerful, inspirational and written from a firm biblical perspective, multi-published author Grace Dola Balogun, gives life to others through the power of Jesus Christ who is the Resurrection and the life. This book will open eyes to the amazing and abundant blessings of accepting Jesus Christ as your Lord and Savior, giving keen insight into the Scriptures on the power available to all through the Holy Spirit with an emphasis on aspects of eternal life for the believer.

## I AM THE ETERNAL LIFE

*I Am The Eternal Life:* Encouraging, uplifting and filled with a sound biblical perspective, this book encourages believers and non-believers alike to look to the One that is Jesus Christ, the Son of God, who is the Bread of life and the one who gives eternal life to all who believe in Him. This book gives readers a heavenly perspective on their life, revealing believer's God-given destiny and purpose to all who call on Jesus Christ as their Lord and Savior. The truth of the Gospel and the Good News is eloquently displayed in this delightful and insightful read.

## About the Author

Grace Dola Balogun graduated from Fordham University Graduate School of Religion and Religious Education in the year 2010 with an M.A. in Religion and Religious Education. She has been a prayer mentor and advisor for many Christians of all denominations for many years.

Visit her online at:

www.Gracereligiousbookspublishers.com

Facebook

Twitter @prayersource

To order additional copies of this book, please E-mail: info@gracereligiousbookspublishers.com.

This book may also be ordered from 30,000 wholesalers, retailers, and booksellers in the U. S., and in Canada and over100 countries globally.

To contact Grace Dola Balogun for an interview or a speaking engagement, please E-mail:

info@gracereligiousbookspublishers.com

The Spirit and the bride say,

"Come!" And let the one who hears say, "Come!" Let the

one who is thirsty come;

and let the one who wishes take the free

gift of the water of life (Revelation 22:17).

*MARANATHA EVEN SO COME LORD JESUS (1ST*

*CORINTHIANS 16:22, REVELATION 22:20)*

## ORDER FORM

## TO ORDER YOUR COPY OF ANY BOOK:

NAME:_______________________________________

ADDRESS:____________________________________

___________________________________________

TELEPHONE:__________________________________

FAX#:_______________________________________

MAIL:_______________________________________

QUANTITY:___________________________________

### MAIL TO:

**Grace Religious Books Publishing & Distributors, Inc.
New York
213 Bennett Avenue
New York, NY  10040**

www.ingramcontent.com/pod-product-compliance
Lightning Source LLC
Chambersburg PA
CBHW071021180726
48291CB00004B/1569